What's That Noise?

Contents

A Noisy Start	2
Shhhh! I'm Sleeping	4
Feeling Noise	6
Breaking Glass	8
Lift-off!	10
Under the Sea	12
The Biggest Bang	14
Making a Noise	16

Chloe Rhodes
Character Illustrations by Jon Stuart

www.SteckVaughn.com
800-531-5015

A Noisy Start

We all make noise. We start as soon as we are born.

Noise is measured in decibels. A baby crying is 60 decibels on the noise-o-meter.

That is as loud as my alarm clock!

Shhhh! I'm Sleeping

Some people make noise in their sleep.

Snoring can be 70 decibels on the noise-o-meter.

Feeling Noise

People who are deaf can feel noise. Evelyn Glennie is a deaf musician.

Evelyn's music is 95 decibels on the noise-o-meter.

Noise makes things vibrate. Evelyn Glennie uses vibration to help her play.

Breaking Glass

The human voice makes vibrations. Some singers can break glass with their voices.

Lift-off!

A rocket flying into space makes lots of noise. The engine is so loud it hurts your ears.

Under the Sea

The loudest animal is the blue whale. Whales make noises that can move a long way under the water.

Blue whales can hear each other from very far away.

The Biggest Bang

One of the loudest noises ever heard came from a volcano. The volcano was called Krakatoa (crack-a-toe-a).

Making a Noise